LYM

-9 AUG 20

23 AU

D0505742

THIS BOOK BELONGS TO:

_____

C333648534

To Alice and Matt. T.F

For Arthur Richard Cowling. R.B

This paperback first published in 2014 by Andersen Press Ltd.,
First published in Great Britain in 2013 by Andersen Press Ltd.,
20 Vauxhall Bridge Road, London SW1V 2SA.
Published in Australia by Random House Australia Pty.,
Level 3, 100 Pacific Highway, North Sydney, NSW 2060.
Text copyright © Toby Forward, 2013.
Illustration copyright © Ruth Brown, 2013.
The rights of Toby Forward and Ruth Brown to be identified
as the author and illustrator of this work have been asserted
by them in accordance with the
Copyright, Designs and Patents Act, 1988.
All rights reserved.
Colour separated in Switzerland by Photolitho AG, Zürich.
Printed and bound in Malaysia by Tien Wah Press.

10   9   8   7   6   5   4   3   2   1

British Library Cataloguing in Publication Data available.
ISBN 978 1 78344 104 4

MIX
Paper from
responsible sources
FSC® C012700
FSC
www.fsc.org

The Quayside Cat

Toby Forward & Ruth Brown

ANDERSEN PRESS

When the sea sucks back from the harbour wall and the sunlight strokes the cobbled streets the quayside cat, Jim, comes to talk with Old Tregarn about his days long ago at sea.

They look out at the tall ships and
Tregarn tells his tales:

"Rats as big as chickens.
Big as I was, some of them.
I picked them off, and shook
them by the neck.

Once a crew of pirates
hove alongside and
boarded us. The fighting
went on all day
and half the night.

But the storms . . .
When the winds picked up,
those were the times to
watch yourself. The deck
sloped like a church roof
and no man could stand."

"I'd love to be a ship's cat like you," says Jim.
"But 'tis a hard life aboard."
"You make it so exciting."
"It was. But where there's excitement,
there's danger."
"Tell me another story."
"Tomorrow. I'm tired.
Look, the sun's almost gone."

"But I want to go aboard and feel the deck move and stand under the sails when they fill with wind. I want to feel the tip and rock of the ship."

"You want the safe earth beneath your paws," replies Old Tregarn. "You want your whiskers in fresh milk every day and a fire to curl up by. Don't go to sea. Go home."

"No," says Jim. "I'm going tonight. Take me aboard. Show me."

Old Tregarn sees a boat going out to the ship.
"Come on, then," he says, "let's jump aboard."
The water lifts the boat. Rise and fall. Gentle
harbour sway. Jim presses close to Old Tregarn.
"Is it always like this?"

"Ssssh. At sea the waves
are as big as hills. Tall as
the steeple."

The boat ties alongside and, when
all is clear, they jump aboard.

Jim stares up at the mast,
disappearing into the night.
The rigging soars above him.
"Quickly, come below,"
says Old Tregarn.

Below decks, Jim presses
close to Old Tregarn.

"It's not how I thought it
would be," says Jim.
"Do you really like it?"
"Once you've loved the sea,
you'll always love her."
A rat runs over the barrel of a cannon and
drops by Jim. The biggest rat he's ever seen.
"Face 'em down, lad."
"I want to go home," says Jim.
"Too late. Hark to that rattle. That's the anchor,
lad. We're leaving harbour on the night tide."

Jim runs up and stares over the side.
They're on the open sea.
"Look," says Tregarn, "dolphins.
Watch them play and follow us."

"I wish I could swim," says Jim, "but it's
so rough, I can't even stand up."
"A pleasant swell. You'll learn to love it."

Jim hides in a corner and
puts his head against the
timbers and is sick. Old
Tregarn puts his face to
the wind and purrs.

The morning comes and Charlie the cabin boy makes a fuss
of Jim, and feeds him scraps of fish and meat. He puts Jim
in his pocket and climbs to the top of the mast.

"I've never seen a seagull so close."
"Careful," says Charlie. "They've got sharp beaks."
"I wish I could fly," says Jim.

"It was wonderful," he tells
Old Tregarn. "I could see for ever.
The sea goes all the way to the sky."
"Did you look out for pirates?"
"Oh yes."
"And were you frightened?"
"Not a bit."
"Then let's go up together tomorrow."
"Er, once is enough. We might
be in the way."

At night they dance and feast.
Jim gets tangled in the cabin boy's legs
and they all laugh.

The storms come and the ship rides the waves.
As high as steeples. Higher.

The sails become so threadbare that when the crew
hoists them, they catch just enough wind to move
her through the water, gently, as a father takes a
child and leads it to safety.

After the storm, the silence of the night at sea.
"When can we go home?" asks Jim.
"When the ship returns," replies Tregarn. "She's a good old ship, but the tackle and rig are old as well."

The timbers creak. The deck splits.
The sails are little more than lace tablecloths.
"They'll no more catch the wind than a net
catches water," says Old Tregarn. "Can we save her?"
"She's too far gone to sail properly. She's taking in water
as fast as they can bale her out."
"Shall we drown?"
Old Tregarn looks at the tattered sails.
"Perhaps they'll hold."

"We're home," cries Jim, as the
village hoves into sight. A pile of old sail cloth
lies folded by the bulkhead. Old Tregarn curls up
and sinks into the white, frayed folds.
"Let's go now," says Jim.
"You go," replies Old Tregarn. "The boats are taking the crew ashore."
"Come on then."

Old Tregarn strokes his cheek against
the weather-beaten sail.
"One last voyage for me. I've had enough of land."
"But the tide's on the turn."
"Better go ashore then, Jim."

Still the sea sucks back from the harbour wall and still the sunlight strokes the cobbled streets, and now the quayside cat, Old Jim, looks out at the tall ships and tells his tales about his days long ago at sea.

"You make it so exciting."
"It was," Jim smiles and watches until
only the sunbeams on the sea remain.

ALSO BY TOBY FORWARD AND RUTH BROWN:

9781842705834

'Brilliant. A very special book indeed.'
DAILY MAIL

'Superbly observed' SUNDAY TIMES